For Jonathan, Mark, and Alexandra Cappozzola, with love
—E. M.

To Pamela and Alec, with love
—B. A.

Rabbit Ears Books is an imprint of Rabbit Ears Productions, Inc.
Published by Simon & Schuster, Inc.
1230 Avenue of the Americas
New York, New York 10020

Manufactured in the United States of America
10 9 8 7 6 5 4 3 2 1

Library of Congress Cataloging-in-Publication Data

Metaxas, Eric.
Pinocchio / written by Eric Metaxas ; illustrated by Brian Ajhar.
p. cm.
Summary: Pinocchio, a wooden puppet full of tricks and mischief, with a talent
for getting into and out of trouble, wants more than anything to become a real boy.
ISBN 0-689-80230-7
[1. Puppets—Fiction. 2. Fairy tales.] I. Ajhar, Brian, ill.
II. Collodi, Carlo, 1826–1890. Avventure di Pinocchio. English. III. Title.
PZ8.M55Pi 1996
[E]—dc20   95-8578
CIP   AC

EDITOR'S NOTE: THE AUDIOCASSETTE ACCOMPANYING THIS BOOK IS A THEATRICAL RENDITION
AND DOES NOT EXACTLY MATCH THE TEXT IN THE BOOK.

Pinocchio

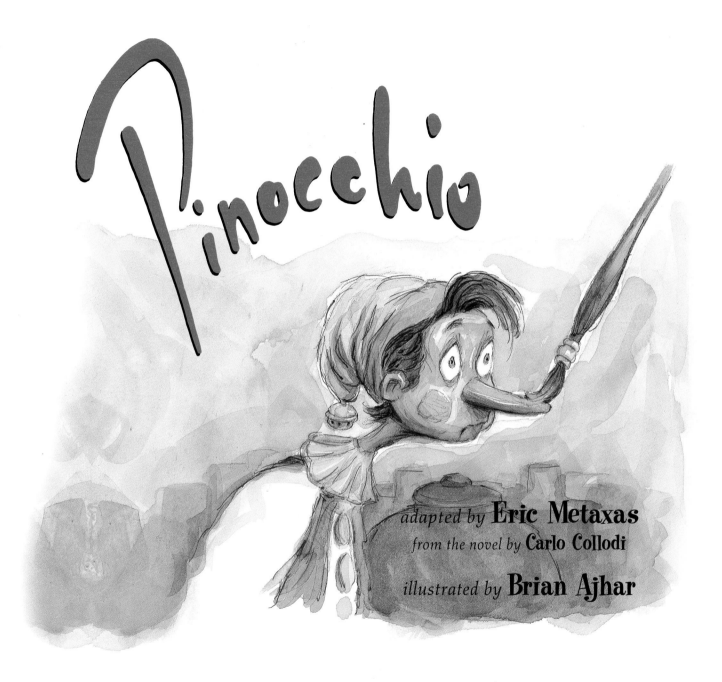

adapted by **Eric Metaxas**
from the novel by **Carlo Collodi**

illustrated by **Brian Ajhar**

· Rabbit Ears Books ·

Once upon a time there lived a lonely toy maker named Geppetto. One rainy day as he was daydreaming about what it might be like to have a child of his own, Geppetto began carving a small wooden puppet. And except for the single outstanding feature of a magnificently long nose, which made him look somewhat mischievous, the puppet looked very much like a little boy, indeed.

Just as Geppetto was putting the final touches on him, though, the puppet leaped away from him, ran across the room, and jumped out of the open window as fleet-footed as a rabbit.

Geppetto did not pause to wonder at the miracle that had just taken place; he only jumped up and ran after the puppet, crying, "Pinocchio! Pinocchio!"

When he reached the town square, a policeman, seeing Geppetto carrying his knife and chasing the little boy, thought he meant the boy harm. And so he arrested Geppetto and took him away to jail.

Now Pinocchio, having nowhere else to go, returned to Geppetto's cottage. Immediately he became involved in a conversation with a black cricket. The cricket warned him that he mustn't be mischievous and that he should obey his father, Geppetto.

But Pinocchio only laughed at this. "I'd prefer to obey myself," he said. "You see, I'd much rather play and amuse myself morning, noon, and night."

"But, don't you realize," said the cricket, "that if you do that you will end up being a perfect jackass?"

This bit of wisdom did not please Pinocchio, however, and so he threw a wooden mallet at the cricket and chased it away.

"A perfect jackass, indeed!" he said. "Humph! What does a stupid cricket know?"

Pinocchio then lay down in front of the fireplace and fell sound asleep. But when he awoke he saw that his wooden feet had been burned to mere ashes. He was beside himself. How could he have been so stupid?

Just then Geppetto returned. Immediately Pinocchio said he was sorry, and promised that if Geppetto carved a new pair of feet for him he would never run away again. "And I promise to go to school and be a good boy. I've learned my lesson." Well, this sounded reasonable enough to Geppetto, and so he set out carving Pinocchio a new pair of feet.

And the very next morning Pinocchio set off for school, resolved to be a good boy.
On the way, however, he passed a marionette theater and, unable to resist, crept in
to watch.

The stage was full of puppets who were in the middle of a magnificent performance. But the moment they recognized a fellow puppet in the audience, they stopped the performance and invited him onto the stage. The audience began to jeer and boo, for they wanted the performance to continue.

Now, this attracted the attention of the puppet master, who became very angry. He grabbed Pinocchio and said he would use him to feed the fire cooking his supper. Pinocchio and the other puppets begged the puppet master to spare his life, and in time, because the puppet master had a big heart, he let Pinocchio go. Why, the big fellow even gave him six pieces of gold as a going-away present. Pinocchio skipped away happily, for not only had his life been spared, but he was now a very rich boy.

Along the road, however, he soon met a fox and a cat. "Good day to you!" they said to Pinocchio, acting very friendly. Pinocchio was easily taken in by their charm and, eager to reciprocate, he foolishly told them all about the puppet master and his six gold coins.

"Well," said the fox with a big smile, thinking of all the roasted partridge he could buy with six gold coins. "I know of a place where if you plant your golden coins into the ground, they grow into great trees that bear golden coins for fruit. You'll be the richest man in all of Italy!"

Now Pinocchio knew he should find his way to school, but he could not resist the fox's persuasive words, and so he accompanied the fox and cat on the road to the magical place they had spoken of.

They still had not reached it by nightfall, though, so the fox suggested they spend the night at a nearby tavern called the Red Lobster. Pinocchio was so far from home he didn't know what to do and so he went inside.

At dinner the fox and the cat ordered enough food for twenty-five foxes and thirty-nine cats. After they ate every morsel, they went to bed.

In the morning Pinocchio awoke to find that the fox and cat had gone, and they had left him to pay their enormous bill.

The innkeeper gave Pinocchio a note from the cat:

Dear Woodenhead,
We had to leave suddenly as my eldest son has come down with a case of the chilblains and looks to be in bad shape.
Meet us at the magic Field this Afternoon.
The Cat

What could Pinocchio do? He paid the gigantic bill, which was one gold piece, and continued alone on the road to the magic field.

But as he was walking along, two robbers, who looked strangely familiar, came after him. He ran for his life, as fast as his wooden legs would carry him, but the robbers continued chasing him. Finally, he came to a house. Huffing and puffing, he knocked on the door.

The occupant of the house was a fairy with blue hair. She agreed to hide Pinocchio, and when the assassins came to the door she told them she'd seen a puppet running off along the road only moments before. And so they disappeared.

"Thank you so much, Miss Blue Fairy," said Pinocchio. "You saved my life!"

"What did you have that they wanted to steal?" she asked him.

"Oh, nothing," he replied. "I had some coins, but I lost them as I was running."

On telling this lie, however, Pinocchio's wooden nose grew two inches.

"Where?" she asked.

"In the woods over there." Again his nose grew.

"Are you sure?" she asked.

"Absolutely!" he said, and with this his nose suddenly shot out ten feet so that he couldn't move his head this way or that.

"You shouldn't lie," the blue fairy said.

Well, Pinocchio saw the folly of his lying all too clearly. It was, in fact, as plain as the nose on his face.

"You're right," he said. "I am sorry." And he was. With that, a dozen brightly colored woodpeckers flew in through the window and in a flurry reduced his nose to its former size. This made Pinocchio very happy.

"Thanks again!" he said. "How can I ever repay you?"

"Just go straight home," she said. "That will be thanks enough."

Pinocchio eagerly nodded in agreement. But even with this simple gesture his nose grew a few inches because in his heart he meant to try and find the magic field, and not go straight home. But he turned around quickly to hide this and set off along the road.

Now almost immediately he bumped into the fox and cat again. "Ah, how are your eldest son's chilblains?" Pinocchio asked the cat.

"Chilblains?" the cat said. "Eldest son? Oh! Oh, yes! His recovery was rather . . . unbelievable! Thank you so much for asking."

In time the trio came to the aforementioned field. It did not look very magical to Pinocchio, but he planted his sack of five coins anyway and then he and the cat and fox went off to wait for the tree to grow. But Pinocchio was very tired from his adventures and so, as he was waiting, he fell asleep.

But when he awoke, the fox and the cat were gone. He quickly ran to the place where he'd planted his money, but, alas, no money tree had grown. Pinocchio was very disappointed. *That settles it*, he thought to himself. *I'll dig up my five remaining coins and go straight home. I've learned my lesson. I'm a bad boy indeed!*

But when Pinocchio dug up the sack he found that it was empty. *I'm a very bad boy,* he thought. *I shall have to ask Geppetto's forgiveness. I've caused him a great deal of worrying, and now I don't even have a sack of gold to show for it.*

When Pinocchio finally got home, however, he saw that Geppetto was no longer there. Just then a robin, who had been watching Pinocchio, spoke up.

"Geppetto is not here," the robin said. "When you did not return he grew so distraught that he went to sea looking for you."

This overwhelmed Pinocchio. "I'm the worst boy in the world! I must find him. Where has he sailed from?" he asked the robin.

"The place is many, many miles from here," the robin said. "But I can take you. Hop on my back." And so Pinocchio hopped on the bird's downy back and they were off.

The bird flew higher and higher into the sky. At last the robin landed on the very seashore where Geppetto had set off on his journey. Several fishermen told Pinocchio the direction in which Geppetto had piloted his raft. Thanking the robin, Pinocchio leaped into the waves and, as buoyant as a cork, swam out in the direction of Geppetto's boat.

Pinocchio swam all night long, but he did not see Geppetto. Then there was a terrible storm and in time, Pinocchio realized that Geppetto must have drowned. Finally Pinocchio swam to a distant shore and, exhausted, he fell asleep.

But when he awoke he saw that he was not far from the cottage of the blue fairy. He approached the door and she answered.

"Please help me," Pinocchio said. "I am sick and tired of being a puppet and I am weary of these terrible adventures I've been having. And the worst of it is that now I've learned that my father, Geppetto, is gone forever. Please let me stay with you. I promise to be good and to go to school. I promise!"

Well, the blue fairy could see that Pinocchio was sincere and, taken with Pinocchio's grief for his father, she agreed to let him stay with her in the cottage.

And so the next morning, Pinocchio set off on the road to school, resolved to behave himself from that time on. And this time he did behave himself, and as a result, things in school went splendidly that day. And they went splendidly the next day as well. And the day after that, too.

In no time several months had passed and Pinocchio had become a model pupil. He had performed so well in school, in fact, that at the end of the semester the blue fairy took Pinocchio aside and informed him that she would give him a special party the very next day to celebrate. She instructed Pinocchio to invite all of his friends and so he set out into the village, happy as can be.

As he walked along the road, though, he bumped into a tall, lanky classmate of his nicknamed Lucignolo. When Pinocchio told him about the party, Lucignolo rubbed his jaw.

"That's too bad about this party of yours," he said.

Pinocchio did not understand. "What do you mean 'that's too bad'?"

"Well you see," said Lucignolo, "I'm going to a place called the Land of No School and won't be able to make it. It will be a party every day, every night, every moment. Just think of it! And a golden coach will be here to take me any moment. It will be *fantastico*!"

Well, Lucignolo painted such a convincing picture of the endless fun they would have at the Land of No School that Pinocchio's wooden mouth just hung open. He knew that he couldn't go, but he'd never felt so tempted in his entire life.

"Surely this silly party could be postponed," Lucignolo said. "You've been such a good student. That deserves a reward, doesn't it? Even the blue fairy would agree. She was the one who wanted you to have a celebration in the first place, and what is the Land of No School but one big celebration? You simply must come along."

Well, that seemed to make sense. In fact, it made perfect sense. Pinocchio knew the blue fairy wouldn't mind. Of course she wouldn't! And so, just like that, it was settled. When the golden coach arrived, pulled by twelve sad-looking donkeys, Pinocchio and Lucignolo stepped aboard, and before they could find a seat, the gilded coach lurched forward and they were off.

At last they arrived at the Land of No School and indeed there was no school to be seen anywhere, only endless games and amusements and cakes and lollipops—in short, everything a child would want!

Pinocchio started right in on having fun. It was truly more fun than he could take in, just as Lucignolo had said.

At length, however, Pinocchio grew tired. Since there was no bedtime in this wonderful land, Pinocchio climbed into the highest branches of a great tree and went to sleep. But all through the night he dreamed of that horrid black cricket in Geppetto's workshop who'd said that if he followed his own inclinations to amuse himself morning, noon, and night, he'd become a perfect jackass. And in his dream he had, indeed, become a jackass.

When at last he awoke, Pinocchio was glad he'd only been dreaming and he climbed down and immediately cast about for some game he might play.

When he walked past a fun house and looked at himself in one of the distorting mirrors, it looked as though he had donkey's ears! He laughed at this. But even his laugh sounded like a donkey's laugh. And now, when Pinocchio touched his ears, they even felt long and furry, just like a donkey's. What was happening? He turned away from the mirror, but even so he continued to bray like a perfect jackass, and in the next moment he had a complete set of hooves and then a long tail.

Then, before Pinocchio knew what was happening, he found himself being herded onto a train car filled with other donkeys. Pinocchio cried and cried. When at last the train stopped, Pinocchio was taken off and sold to a circus trainer, and for the next several weeks he was taught how to be a performing circus donkey.

When the time for the grand performance came, Pinocchio was so sad that he could not bring himself to perform any of the tricks he'd learned. He cried, but it only came out like a donkey's braying. The trainer became furious and he angrily sold Pinocchio to one of the circus hands, who decided to kill the useless donkey and use his skin to make a drum.

What's more, the circus hand decided that the easiest way to do this was by drowning, so he led Pinocchio to the edge of a cliff by the sea and pushed him over.

Pinocchio fell and fell, splashing at last into the deep water. A large school of fish swarmed around Pinocchio and ate away at the donkey until there was nothing left but the wooden puppet he had been before. Immediately he popped to the surface like a cork and began swimming away as fast as he could.

But his adventures weren't over yet, for right behind him there was a horrible sea monster several miles long! And upon seeing Pinocchio, it immediately swallowed him up.

Suddenly Pinocchio found himself deep in the belly of the endless sea monster. It was dark. It was as dark as midnight. But far in the distance Pinocchio spotted a pinprick of light. He began making his way toward it.

It was Geppetto! Pinocchio's joy on seeing his old father, Geppetto, was only equaled by Geppetto's joy on seeing his long-lost son. They danced around and around and around, beside themselves with happiness.

When at last they caught their breath, Pinocchio related his adventures. Then Geppetto related how he'd been out on a raft looking for Pinocchio when the sea monster swallowed him. For more than two years he had been inside the vast creature, living off the contents of a large ship in its belly. But now the food was nearly gone and they would surely perish.

But Pinocchio could not be discouraged. "We will swim out of here," he said. "I am made of very buoyant wood, as you yourself know very well. Hold on to me and we will be all right."

And so they made their way slowly to the mouth of the ancient sea monster, who had fallen asleep. They quietly swam out past the glistening pilings of sharp teeth and into the ocean.

Pinocchio swam for many miles. At length they came upon a silver tuna fish who offered them a ride. When they arrived onshore they thanked the fish and, tired and waterlogged, they made their way back to Geppetto's old shop. Exhausted, they fell soundly asleep.

When Pinocchio awoke in the morning he discovered something that took his breath away. For, you see, Pinocchio was no longer a puppet, but was now a real boy. A real boy!

He immediately woke Geppetto, who rubbed his eyes, unable to believe what they told him. Geppetto's and Pinocchio's joy was so powerful that they just sat and stared at each other for many hours without saying a single word.

And had it not been for their hunger, which forced them to get up and find some breakfast, they would be sitting there still.